Dunc's Dump

OTHER YEARLING BOOKS YOU WILL ENJOY:

THE COOKCAMP, *Gary Paulsen*
THE BOY WHO OWNED THE SCHOOL, *Gary Paulsen*
THE VOYAGE OF THE *FROG, Gary Paulsen*
HOW TO EAT FRIED WORMS, *Thomas Rockwell*
HOW TO FIGHT A GIRL, *Thomas Rockwell*
HOW TO GET FABULOUSLY RICH, *Thomas Rockwell*
MAKE LIKE A TREE AND LEAVE, *Paula Danziger*
EVERYONE ELSE'S PARENTS SAID YES, *Paula Danziger*
RAT TEETH, *Patricia Reilly Giff*
MATTHEW JACKSON MEETS THE WALL, *Patricia Reilly Giff*

YEARLING BOOKS/YOUNG YEARLINGS/YEARLING CLASSICS are designed especially to entertain and enlighten young people. Patricia Reilly Giff, consultant to this series, received her bachelor's degree from Marymount College and a master's degree in history from St. John's University. She holds a Professional Diploma in Reading and a Doctorate of Humane Letters from Hofstra University. She was a teacher and reading consultant for many years, and is the author of numerous books for young readers.

For a complete listing of all Yearling titles,
write to Dell Readers Service,
P.O. Box 1045, South Holland, IL 60473.

Gary Paulsen

Dunc's Dump

A YEARLING BOOK

Published by
Dell Publishing
a division of
Bantam Doubleday Dell Publishing Group, Inc.
666 Fifth Avenue
New York, New York 10103

The trademark Yearling® is registered in the U.S. Patent and
Trademark Office.

The trademark Dell® is registered in the U.S. Patent and
Trademark Office.

ISBN: 0-440-40762-1

Printed in the United States of America

March 1993

10 9 8 7 6 5 4 3 2 1

OPM

Dunc's Dump

Chapter · 1

Amos Binder held the two test tubes up to the light. "Yellow and blue," he said. "If I mix them, I should get green."

Dunc Culpepper, Amos's best friend for life, looked up from a newspaper he had spread on Amos's bed. They were in Amos's room, which always looked like a disaster area—unlike Dunc's room, which was always neat. Dunc put the paper down. "I don't think that's what your parents had in mind when they gave you the chemistry set—making colors."

"What do you mean?"

"Your grades in science. I was here the day

1

your dad said they were in the toilet. They gave you the set so you could understand science, not play color games."

"Melissa," Amos said.

"What?"

"Melissa. She likes colors."

Amos would have died for Melissa Hansen, thought the sun rose and set on Melissa Hansen, thought his very heart beat and would always beat for Melissa Hansen. Melissa Hansen didn't know he was alive.

"What are you talking about?" Dunc put the paper down in the only clear spot on the bed—between a half-finished model dinosaur and an almost-used piece of pizza. "What do you mean Melissa likes colors?"

"I overheard Janey Halverson tell Rebecca Bisgaard that she heard Janice Blitzer talking to her brother—you know, the one they call Garbage Can because of how he eats, except not to his face because he can unscrew your head . . ."

"Amos."

". . . and she said, Janice to Garbage Can, that she heard her best friend tell her *other*

2

best friend that she knew Melissa Hansen liked to wear colorful clothes."

Dunc waited, but Amos didn't say anything more.

"That's it?" Dunc asked.

Amos nodded.

"From that you think Melissa likes colors?"

Amos nodded again. "It's just logical, isn't it?"

"And you think that if you know about colors Melissa will like you?"

"It's a start. All I have to do is learn about colors. I can see it all now. I'll be walking down the hall and Melissa will meet me and she'll be wearing something with, you know, colors in it and I'll look at it and I'll say, you know, that I know about colors and then she'll like me because I know about colors and I'll ask her to go bike riding with me and while we're riding . . ."

"Amos, it's getting away from you again."

". . . I'll ask her if she wants to go to a movie sometime, and she'll say yes, and it's all, Dunc, all because I know about colors. Now watch while I pour this yellow into the blue and get green."

"Amos, what are you mixing there?"

"I don't know. Just some things that came with the chemistry set. They had names on them, but I was more interested in the colors."

"Do you think it's a good idea to mix them without knowing what they are?"

"I know what they are—they're blue and yellow. And I know if I mix them I get green."

"Amos—"

"Watch."

Amos held up the yellow test tube and carefully poured the entire contents of the blue test tube into the yellow.

The results were immediate.

There was a loud *whuummph* kind of sound, like a large belch, and the room was instantly filled with a huge, packed cloud of green fog-smoke that smelled like a cross between rotten eggs and a skunk that's been dead on the highway for about a month.

"Fire!" Amos yelled, choked, and ran for the door—or for where he thought the door ought to be. He missed by a good six feet and plowed into the dresser, where his entire collection of soccer bubble-gum cards was stored. "Fire!"

Dunc dropped to all fours. There was an open area there about six inches high, and by laying his head down sideways, he could get a breath and see clearly. "There's no fire, Amos. Just get down on your face, and we can crawl out."

Amos bounced off the dresser twice more before falling down and finding the clear area. Dunc was ahead of him by this time and had crawled to the door and had it open. The cloud, which had been getting thicker and stinkier all the time, was suddenly free and rushed out of the room into the hallway, down the stairs, into the living room, and spilled into the kitchen, where it swirled around the corner and caught Amos's mother as she was taking a sip of coffee.

"Amos!" she croaked just before the stink took her down, spilling coffee on her new realty suit as she crawled for the doorway and fresh air. "Amos, you get down here right now!"

Chapter·2

"It could have been worse." Amos put the sponge back in the bucket of warm water and rinsed it before squeezing it out and wiping the walls. "They didn't ground me at all this time. Remember when I ran across the rug with the lawn mower that time? Dad grounded me until I was eighty-four. But all we have to do now is clean up the mess."

Dunc paused in his wiping. The green fog had left a soft slime on all the walls. It looked bad, but it wiped off fairly easily. "And do a project for science at school. Something to bring your grade up."

Amos nodded. "That, too—but they wanted

7

me to do that anyway. I figure we got off fairly easy, all in all."

"I'm not sure why I'm helping at all." Dunc was wiping again. "I didn't mix the junk up."

"Because you're my best friend for life," Amos said, "and because I would do the same for you if you tried to make colors and it got away from you."

"I suppose you want me to help on the science project too."

"Let me put it this way. You know how much I know about science, and I know how much you know about science. I vote for using you. How do you vote?"

Dunc nodded. "I agree."

"So what are we going to do?"

Dunc frowned, thinking, his sponge stopped for a moment. "Something was in the paper—"

"Oh, no. Not that."

"Not what?"

"The paper. You read the paper and get us into things."

"No I don't."

"What about the ring of monkeys stealing toilets? You started that with the paper."

"Well . . ."

"And I wound up with a toilet on my head."

"Not this time. This was something else, something I read about the environment. Oh, yeah, I remember now. Somebody is polluting the garbage."

Amos stopped wiping. "I must have heard wrong. I thought you said somebody was polluting the garbage."

"I did."

Amos stared at him. "I had a cousin once who held his breath until he turned blue because his mother wouldn't buy him candy. He says things like that, like 'Don't pollute the garbage.' Have you been holding your breath?"

"No—it's not like that. Somebody really *is* polluting the garbage."

"How can you? Isn't garbage already, you know, polluted?"

"Well, there's garbage and there's garbage, isn't there? Some of it's worse than other types, and they've been finding a lot of strange garbage in the dump."

Amos sighed. "Only you, Dunc—in all the

world, only you would know what's going on at the dump."

Dunc rose up on his toes. "I make it my business to know things, and the dump is one of the things I know about."

"All right, all right. So there's weird garbage at the dump. How does that become a science project for school?"

Dunc smiled. "Simple. It's like any other case. We just find out who's polluting the dump, and then you do a paper on it."

"Other case?" Amos turned. "What do you mean, other ca—"

He was going to say more, but the phone rang.

One clear ring.

And no matter what Amos was doing or saying, when he heard a phone ring, he had to answer it by the end of that all-important first ring because he was certain, absolutely positive, that it was Melissa trying to call him, and if he didn't make it on the first ring, she would hang up.

There were phones located throughout Amos's house. After having been trampled several times, even his older sister—who called him things with the word *butt* in them, like butthead and buttface and buttbreath—had voted to have a phone in nearly every room.

But they were working on the walls in the entry hall.

And there was no phone there.

There were, however, two half-filled pails of warm soapy water positioned one slightly forward of the other, approximately thirty-five centimeters apart—in short, the perfect distance for what was about to happen.

Amos was the world expert on phone rings, and as he had told Dunc perhaps two thousand times, the ring can be broken down into a series of sound pulses. There were between sixteen and twenty-two sound pulses in each ring, depending on the type of phone, but the exact number didn't matter. What counted was the first four pulses.

On the first pulse the feet had to be moving, right foot first, driving down, and by the second pulse the left foot had to be starting its upswing to come down and power the speed up. At the same time the arms had to come up in the classic form, the head back, the tongue

11

out the side of the mouth, nostrils flared—without all these ingredients, it was impossible to make the phone by the end of the first ring.

On the first pulse of this ring, Amos was nearly perfect. Instantly, when the ring started, his mind calculated the exact distance to the nearest phone—seven point three nine meters to the phone hanging on the kitchen wall—and the right foot came down, the left up, his arms raised, nostrils flared, tongue out, a bit of spit flying from the end. Absolutely classic.

It was during the second and third pulses that things started to go horribly wrong.

The left foot came up, powered down like a driving piston, and would have moved his body correctly.

Except.

With amazing accuracy, as if it had cross hairs and a scope, the left foot came down in the center of Dunc's bucket of warm soapy water. And even here it would have been possible to avoid disaster if Amos had only had smaller feet. But his tennis shoe was the exact size needed to cause his foot to jam down and stick hard in the bottom.

Approximately three-tenths of a second later his right foot came down and with the same accuracy jammed into the other bucket of warm soapy water and the potential disaster was complete.

Had he been able to stop, there would still have been time to avoid complete catastrophe. But his weight was forward of his movement, his arms were pumping, and his brain was centered on one thing.

The phone.

Later, Dunc said it looked like a nuclear device had detonated in a soap factory.

His momentum carried Amos four quick, choppy steps, his feet acting like plungers in the buckets, turning them to foam that flew around him, ahead of him, behind him in a wild spray that covered everything, blinding Amos, smearing the walls, floor, ceiling as he propelled his way into the kitchen.

And even here there was a slight chance to at least lessen the damage.

Had Amos caught the phone, it might have stopped him, or at least turned him.

But he was blinded by the soap foam that clouded around him, and he missed the phone by a good three centimeters.

Which allowed him to drive straight into the kitchen, aimed at the kitchen table.

Where his mother was sitting looking at an antique glass fishbowl she had just purchased. She looked up just as Amos—or the cloud containing Amos—came barreling in through the kitchen door.

By this time, Amos was starting to fall, tripped by the buckets, and his head came down at the exact angle to drive into the fishbowl.

Still moving well, he bounced off the side of his mother, tipping her chair backward, past her and out into the porch, through the porch, where he carried the screen door off and somersaulted into the back yard, where he finally emerged as a large white cloud topped by a glass-enclosed head, causing their neighbor—an old man named Clarian who sometimes drank red wine during the day—to call the police and report a "UFO man."

Dunc helped Amos pull the fishbowl off his head—luckily there was still enough soap to

14

make his ears slide easily—and pulled Amos to his feet.

"What do you think," Amos said. "Too much speed when I hit the kitchen?"

Dunc nodded. "Yeah—but good form. Absolutely classic."

Chapter·3

"It'll be like a commando raid," Dunc said. "I saw this old movie on television about the Second World War where these guys get into dark clothes and make a raid on some radar installations."

Amos shook his head. "You're gone. Completely gone."

"No, really—"

"Dunc, you're talking about going to the dump after dark to collect samples of garbage."

"So you have to use your imagination a little bit, that's all."

"That isn't all you have to do. This is a

dump, not a radar station. There are rats out there as big as Ford Fiestas, just waiting for somebody to be dumb enough to come into the dump at night."

"We have to go at night—they wouldn't let two kids in there during the day to rummage around through the trash."

Amos shook his head. "I still think it's a bad idea."

But he was weakening, and Dunc felt it. "It's the only way to do this—you'll get a good grade in science, and we'll crack the case of the errant trash."

"What?"

"I'm going to name this the case of the errant trash."

"Name what?"

"This whole case."

"It's not a case, Dunc. It's a science project."

Dunc nodded. "I know, I know. But if it *were* a case, I would name it the case of the errant trash. All the best detectives named their cases like that—you know, later, when they wrote about them."

Amos stared at Dunc for a long time, then

shook his head and sighed. "I think you've gone too far on this one. If I didn't need a good science grade, I'd walk out this door right now."

But he didn't go. They were in Dunc's room where Dunc kept all his "equipment"—black sweatshirts and stocking caps and a small flashlight—that he used when they needed to work at night.

Dunc looked at his watch, which told the exact time, date, and elapsed time in the mainland United States as well as in Alaska, Asia, and Europe, plus the tide tables in all the major oceans of the world, and—according to Amos, who had an old digital watch that didn't work unless you hit it on a rock—told Dunc when he was hungry as well.

"We have thirty-one minutes, forty seconds until sundown, according to my watch."

"Approximately," Amos said. "Don't you mean approximately?"

"No. Exactly. But it still won't be dark enough to perform our mission."

"Don't do that. Don't say things like 'case' or 'mission' anymore. Every time you say that,

I wind up getting pooped on by bats or forgetting my name."

"Project," Dunc added quickly. "We won't be able to go on our science project until solid dark. There's a half moon tonight, and it won't be too bright, so we should be all right for a go . . ."

Amos winced.

". . . at sunset plus one hour forty-two minutes. Maybe we'd better synchronize our watches."

Amos stared at him.

"Right," Dunc said. "We'll skip that part. Let's go over the plan one more time."

"Dunc—"

"I've written it out as a poem so it will be easy to remember. You remember how well that worked, don't you?"

"Dunc—"

" 'A pocket a pence, over the fence. Oh what a bash, sample the trash. A tin can, a rag, into the bag. We've got it taped, make good our escape. . . .' "

Amos closed his eyes while Dunc droned on and thought: Where's my bat, look at the rat. Oh what a treat, it's eating my seat.

He shuddered. It was going to be a long night.

Chapter · 4

Amos picked his foot up gingerly and tried not to throw up. He couldn't help it. Every time he stepped on something soft, he wanted to throw up, and there seemed to be about a million soft things to step on. Soft and runny things. Soft and runny things that smelled really bad.

The problem was, it was so dark.

Dunc had been right. The moon was half full, and it should have given them some light, but the clouds had come in just at sunset and blocked the moon completely.

By the time they had arrived, dressed in dark clothes, at the fence surrounding the town dump, it was so dark, Amos couldn't tell if he was seeing or not seeing.

It was as dark as the inside of a dead cow, Amos thought—sure there must be several of them around. His brain ran on automatic. As dark as the inside of a *really* dead cow. A cow that's been dead at least a week under a hot sun with flies and maggots.

He stopped thinking, swallowed, and tried not to breathe.

Getting over the fence had not been as simple as "a pocket a pence, over the fence." It was an eight-foot-tall chain link fence with three strands of barbed wire on the top, tipping out, and by the time they'd gotten over the wire, Amos felt as if he'd lost at least a pound of flesh.

Dunc had the flashlight but didn't want to use it for fear they would be seen—although Amos couldn't believe there was anybody to see them. It wasn't as if there were a guard on the dump.

Something grabbed at his left leg, held it back. Amos stopped, reached down to push whatever it was away, and felt a familiar shape.

For a moment he couldn't place it. He touched it with his hand, felt the sides of it, and realized suddenly that he was touching fingers, touching a hand.

"Dunc . . ."

"Shh. Remember the poem—'to avoid a fright, stay still and quiet.'"

"Dunc . . ."

Dunc turned. "Stay *quiet!*"

"Dunc, there's a hand holding my leg."

"What?"

"A body, there's a body, somebody's body right down here, holding my left leg, and you just tell me to shut up, and I can't stop talking, you ninny, because there's a body, a really really *real* body, down here holding me, and I think I'm going to blow chow now—"

Dunc flicked the light on momentarily and jumped when he found himself looking at a nude body. Then he looked at it a bit more closely. "Take it easy, Amos—it's just a department store dummy."

Amos was bent over losing everything he'd eaten since he was four years old. "What?"

"It's a dummy—just an old department store dummy. The hand got caught up in your pants leg. You've got to cool it."

"That's easy to say. It wasn't you the dummy grabbed. I just about had a heart attack."

Dunc switched the light on once more, untangled the hand, and turned the light off. "Now come on—we have to get to the new section, where they're dumping now. It's over there."

He set off in the darkness, vanishing instantly in the blackness. Amos held back for an instant, thought about returning to the fence where they'd left their bicycles, but realized he didn't have the slightest idea where it was and set off after Dunc.

Or tried to. He hadn't made a step before his foot caught inside a can and he went down. Face first. In a pile of something not only soft and runny and stinky but that seemed to have life because it stuck to him and wouldn't let go and he promptly lost whatever stomach contents he had somehow retained from the body incident.

He managed to get going again, stumbling

along in the pitch darkness, but inside of three steps he was hopelessly lost.

"Dunc!" he called in a loud whisper.

There was no answer.

"Dunc!"

"What?" Dunc suddenly appeared next to him. "What's the *matter* with you?"

"I'm lost."

"No you're not. You're right here, next to me. And we're in the new garbage."

"We are?"

"Yes. Now help me get samples. Here— take your sack and gather."

Dunc had carried two sacks and he handed one to Amos.

"Tell me again what I'm supposed to gather."

"Garbage. We're in a dump, what do you think we should gather? Roses?"

"How am I going to do it in the dark?"

"By feel."

"You mean *touch* it?"

"Here's a pair of rubber gloves. Now be quiet and get to work."

27

Amos pulled the gloves on and reached down for some garbage to put in his sack.

The first thing he grabbed wiggled and squeaked.

Amos was not quiet.

Chapter · 5

"If my folks come home and find us like this, I'm going to receive capital punishment." Amos glanced over his shoulder at the garage door. "Why didn't we use your garage?"

They were in Amos's garage. It was the next morning, and they had spread the garbage out on the garage floor while Dunc, wearing a white chemist's apron (wouldn't he just, Amos thought), rubber gloves, and using a pair of tongs and a spatula, sampled different bits, which he put in small, sealable sandwich bags.

"I told you." Dunc paused, holding a banana peel that had seen better days with the tongs. "Both your parents work and my mom stays home. We needed privacy for our initial research."

"Don't do that."

"Don't do what?"

"We're playing around in garbage. I'm about to blow chow for the seventh time. Don't call it 'initial research.'"

"But it is, Amos."

"Next you'll be saying, 'It's elementary, my dear Watson.'"

"Well, really, it *is* elementary, Amos."

"No, it's not. It's garbage, that's what it is, and it's starting to smell like a dump in here."

Dunc was back at work. "Just tell them that Scruff tipped the garbage."

Scruff was Amos's dog. Or was the family dog. Years before, in what had become known as the Hot Burrito Incident, Scruff had decided the best thing to do with Amos was spend as much time as possible biting him or chewing up Amos's clothing or—his latest trick—sneaking into Amos's room at night and peeing on Amos's shoes.

"I'd like that." Amos nodded. "I owe Scruff

for ruining my hiking boots. But Mom leaves him in the back yard when she goes to work, and she'd know that I let him in the garage, so I'd catch it anyway." Amos looked at his watch. "Can't you hurry this up?"

"Research is like good soda," Dunc said. "You can't hurry it. When it's right, you drink it."

"That's wine. That's what they say in the wine commercials on television."

"Same thing."

"All right, all right. Just hurry."

"I'm . . . just . . . about . . . done. There. I think I've found something."

"What?"

Dunc held up a Baggie. "This."

Amos leaned close and peered into the sack. "It looks like sugar mixed with something I don't want to think about."

"It's the smell." Dunc unzipped the top of the bag. "Here, try it."

Without thinking, Amos leaned over and took a big noseful from the sack.

"Yaacck!"

Dunc grinned. "Ammonia, right?"

"Yaacck!"

"Perfect. I didn't figure to get that lucky on the first mission. Great."

"Yaacck!"

Chapter · 6

"It's all very simple, really." Dunc held up the book. "Once you know a part of something, you can learn it all."

Amos said nothing. They were back in Dunc's room. It was midmorning, and they had just awakened. Or Amos had. Dunc had apparently been working all night. Amos had told his parents he was sleeping over at Dunc's so they could have more time for "research," as Dunc put it.

Amos had just managed finally to get the stink of ammonia out of his nose and mouth. "Simple," he said, nodding. "Everything is simple to you."

"No, really. You have the stink of ammonia, but it's in powder form. What does that tell you?"

"That somebody has come up with a new kind of stink powder?"

Dunc shook his head. "No, now come on. Think."

"I can't. Smelling that bag burned my brain out."

"It's simple."

"If you say that again, I'm going to brain you."

"Ammonia nitrate. Doesn't that jump into your thoughts?"

Amos stared at him, then shook his head. "Never. Not once in my life has ammonia nitrate jumped into my thoughts."

"Fertilizer."

"Ahh." Amos nodded. "Now *that* has jumped into my thoughts lately. Only under a different name. Especially when I think of you and that bag."

"No. Not like that. Ammonia nitrate is a kind of chemical fertilizer. It's as plain as the nose on your face."

"The nose that *was* on my face, you mean."

"Somebody, person or persons unknown, is dumping chemical fertilizer at the dump."

Amos closed his eyes, sighed, opened them. "Wait now, just wait one minute. You had me out in a dump half a night, grabbing things that moved and made sounds, crawling through stuff that made me vomit, over dead bodies—"

"Department store dummies."

"—or what I *thought* was dead bodies, to tell me that somebody is dumping fertilizer in the dump?"

"Exactly. Perfect, isn't it?"

"Where, please tell me, just where *should* somebody put fertilizer? In the mall?"

Dunc held his hand up. "You don't understand."

"I'm beginning to understand more and more about fertilizer all the time. I think maybe you're *full* of fertil—"

"Not that kind, Amos. Chemicals. Somebody is dumping chemical fertilizer in the dump illegally."

"Oh."

"And all we have to do is catch them and

35

turn them over to the authorities, and that will crack the case."

"You're starting to sound more and more like Sherlock Holmes."

Dunc ignored him. "We'll have it solved in no time. All we have to do is find out who is dumping—trace the garbage back."

"That's the part I'm not really happy about."

"It's all so simple. We just do a little detective work, and you have a science project in the bag."

Amos shook his head. "I'd really rather be working on how to make colors. You know, for Melissa. It seems we got way off the track here. And besides, you haven't said how we'll trace the garbage yet."

"We have to go back to the dump."

"I knew it, I just knew it. At night, right?"

"No. This will be a daylight raid. We'll have to wear deep camouflage, find a way in so we can see which truck dumps which garbage, then follow or ride the truck back to where it came from."

Amos looked at Dunc. For a long time. "You're nuts."

"We can do it."

"We, nothing. I'm not going this time."

"You have to—it's a two-man operation."

"Dunc, listen to me, one more time—it's a dump. It's garbage. It doesn't matter. I want to do colors."

"Environment."

"What?"

"It isn't color that Melissa is interested in. It's the environment."

Amos eyed Dunc suspiciously. "How do you know that?"

"Same as you found out about colors. I heard Billy Dee tell Janey Carlson that he heard Jackie—you know, that kid that always has boogers in his nose—tell Wayne Carlson who told Davonne Washington . . ."

"All right, all right."

". . . that Sarah Kemper said that she heard that Melissa . . ."

"All *right*!"

". . . worries about all the hunting and trapping that goes on and really, really respects someone who cares about the environment and tries to fix it."

Amos sighed. "I'll go."

"I thought you'd see it my way."

"When do we go?"

"This afternoon. As soon as we get our deep camouflage ready."

Chapter · 7

"How do I look?" Dunc stood next to the dump fence and held his arms out.

"Like a large banana peel covered with coffee grounds and boogers and maybe a little baby fertilizer mixed in with—"

"That's enough, Amos."

"I was going to say green runny snot."

"Amos."

"Well, what do you expect when you make me get into an outfit like this?"

Amos was covered with an old half-rotted burlap sack in which Dunc had cut arm and head holes and then wired trash he'd pulled from the trash heaped all around them. Over the top of Amos's head Dunc had jammed an old lampshade and on this he'd hooked other bits of garbage so that Amos was completely covered in refuse from head to toe.

"I can't," Amos muttered, "stand myself."

"Think of Melissa—how proud she'll be."

"It's getting harder and harder to think. The smell is rotting my brain."

Dunc turned away. "Follow me. Stay low, and only move when the trucks and machinery can't see us."

Dunc moved away from the fence between two heaping mountains of what looked to Amos like paper diapers. Amos held back for a moment, then followed.

The town dump was like a large plain covered with trash. It didn't appear to end and there was a haze of smoke and dust over it that made it all seem like a movie set for an alien movie. On the other side, away from where Amos and Dunc had crossed the fence, two huge bulldozers worked like giant monsters pushing the trash that came from the trucks as they brought their garbage-filled Dumpsters, tipped them out, and moved away.

Dunc kept low, and the surprising thing was that he had been right. If they stayed low, moved only when the Caterpillars were headed away from them and the trucks were leaving or turning, they were almost impossible to see.

The boys moved in fits and jerks. When they stopped they looked exactly like garbage and within twenty minutes they were at the bottom of the slope the trucks were dumping over.

Dunc stopped and squatted, motioning with a half-rotted-banana-peel hand for Amos to do the same.

"What now?" Amos asked.

"We wait. When we see a truck that dumps the wrong garbage, we go for it."

Amos tipped the lampshade back a bit so he could peer out at Dunc. "What does that mean, exactly—'go for it'?"

"Just follow my lead. Now be quiet and sit still, and watch up there."

Amos hunkered and peeked up the hill from beneath his lampshade. "It would help if I knew what I was looking for."

"Bad garbage."

41

"Oh. Well, that helps a lot. I was going to look for good garbage."

"Amos."

"It's so easy to tell the difference, you know, here in the dump. There's good garbage and there's bad garbage. . . ."

And he was still talking when a truck backed to the top of the heap and tipped a Dumpster to drop a load down the side of the pile, and Dunc grabbed him by the shoulder, or more correctly the sack, and said in his ear, "There it is! See the powder? Come on, follow me!"

"What?"

But Dunc was halfway up the hill of garbage, scrambling on plastic bags, before Amos could catch up with him.

And then there was no time for talk.

Dunc worked around the freshly dumped load to the still-tipped Dumpster. The driver hadn't even gotten out of the truck and couldn't see around the back, and the men on the tractors were working another pile.

Dunc grabbed the edge of the open Dumpster and swung up and over and in and turned to help Amos.

Amos stopped. "*Inside* the Dumpster?"

"Hurry up!"

Dunc grabbed him by the shoulders and heaved and flipped Amos up and into the Dumpster just as the hydraulic arm started to bring it back up.

The lid closed with a grinding bang.

It was completely dark.

Chapter · 8

"Are you out of your mind?" Amos had to fairly scream to be heard over the sound of the garbage truck's engine. "We can't ride inside a Dumpster!"

"What do you mean, we can't? We're doing it, aren't we?"

And they were, if it could be called riding. The truck bounced with every rut or chuckhole in the road, and there were no springs to absorb the shock inside the Dumpster. The boys bounced from top to bottom, pranging off the steel like rubber balls, and each prang gave a new bruise.

"Ouch!" Amos landed seat first on the cold

steel floor, then shot to the top where he smashed the lampshade so hard down on his head it hit his shoulders. "Mmmmphhh." He spat out a banana peel. "I don't know what we're doing, but I don't think it's riding. People die doing this."

"From what—being in a Dumpster?"

"Yeah. They catch plague and things. It happens all the time."

"No it doesn't. Plague comes from fleas on rats."

"Just the same, just the same—ouch!" Amos slammed into the side wall. "How long do you think we can last?"

Dunc scrabbled his way to the front of the Dumpster, where a faint beam of light came through a tiny hole. He put his eye to the hole. "I don't recognize where we're going—oh, no!"

"What?"

"Nothing."

"What do you mean, nothing? What did you see?"

"Well, nothing, really. I just recognized where we're going."

"Where?"

"I could be wrong, of course. Looking through that little hole. I just saw a corner with a street sign flashing through. It could have been anything."

"If you don't tell me I'm going to take something off my outfit and shove it down your throat."

Dunc hesitated another moment and when Amos was about ready to start for him he gave up. "You remember the parrot?"

"The one that would talk to me only when I swore?"

"Yeah. You remember where he sent us?"

"Sure. Down to the water"—Amos bounced as the truck turned and stopped—"front. You mean we're going to the waterfront?"

The truck engine changed pitch and the Dumpster swung up and out, then dropped to the ground with a thump.

"That's where we're going, the waterfront? Where we blew it apart?"

The truck engine changed again, roared briefly, then grew fainter as the truck drove away.

"Not going," Dunc whispered in the sudden quiet. "I think we're already here."

47

Chapter · 9

Dunc waited another moment, until Amos was standing next to him, and then raised the lid and the two stuck their heads up.

Directly in the face of a man named Charlie Rags. Charlie had seen the truck drop the Dumpster and had decided since it was newly empty—Charlie thought of it as "clean"—he would set up housekeeping. Charlie had once been either a doctor or a flute player—he couldn't remember which. But that was before he had discovered beer, wine, whiskey, cheap wine, and shaving lotion in that order. He had been living in Dumpsters for some years now, drinking what he could get, and would probably have done it for many more years.

"Hello," Dunc said. "Are we close to Fifth Street?"

Dunc and Amos were still in their camouflage. If you looked carefully it was just possible to see an eye or a nose.

But Charlie Rags didn't—indeed, couldn't —look closely. He hadn't been able to look closely at anything for over three decades. His eyes didn't work close. Or far, for that matter.

But he could hear just fine, and he heard Dunc talk. Charlie had heard some strange things talk to him. Bugs, snakes, a lamp pole, and in New York a horse with a policeman sitting on him—the horse said his back was sore—but he had never had garbage open a Dumpster and ask him for directions.

"That way." He pointed, closing one bleary eye. "Two blocks." Then he threw away the wine bottle he was carrying and walked away, swearing never to drink again. Talking garbage was too much.

"Thank you," Dunc said to his back.

Dunc pushed the lid back all the way and climbed out and started walking away.

Amos clambered out of the Dumpster. "Wait a minute—where are you going?"

"Home. We have to hurry and change outfits and come back here after dark."

"We do?"

"Sure. You don't think they'll come in the daylight and leave illegal garbage, do you?"

"No. Of course. It was stupid of me."

"Well, then."

"Of course we have to come back after dark. I should have guessed. It's the waterfront and there are people down here who would sell us for yard ornaments. Of course we have to come after dark. Otherwise it wouldn't be dangerous, would it?"

"You're mumbling," Dunc said over his shoulder. "And don't lose your garbage yet until we get to a bus stop. Nobody will bother us looking like this."

"Seems stupid to me, coming back in the dark, just stupid. . . ."

"You're still mumbling."

"It's the lampshade over my mouth."

"What? I didn't hear you."

"Lampshade."

"Hurry up, will you? The buses come on

51

the hour and we've only got a couple of minutes to make the corner."

Amos ran to catch up, which brought him slightly ahead of Dunc as they reached the corner of Fifth Street where the bus would be.

Later they would argue about Amos's position and how it had caused the disaster. Amos blamed Dunc for yelling at him to hurry up, which caused him to increase speed and put him at the bus stop at the precise moment he needed to be there for the calamity to occur. Dunc said no, things happened with a natural flow, and what happened would have happened anyway, no matter what, but Amos didn't believe it.

The difficulty lay with cellular phones.

Amos had done research on cellular phones, trying to find out just when they had been invented and just exactly why. He did this about the time he wrote the President of the United States and explained just exactly why they should be *un*invented, although he never got an answer.

The problem was his apparently genetic phone-answering code. Anytime a phone rang, anywhere a phone rang, he was convinced that it was Melissa calling. At first it seemed to include almost any bell—causing a memorable catastrophe when his mother's new oven timer went off and Amos destroyed the kitchen trying to answer the oven. It had taken a doctor to get the oven grate off. He had since worked some of the bells out of his system so that he no longer ran for oven timers or children's tricycle bells or the belt beepers worn by doctors.

But it was different with cellular phones.

It is true that he did not often hear them ring. The odds were that if he happened to be near one, it wouldn't ring, and he had only once before actually had a problem with a cellular phone. He had been riding in a car, stopped at traffic, and a phone in the car sitting next to them had rung. Luckily, the man in the car had a twelve-year-old daughter and understood the problem with phones and didn't press charges, but it had been a narrow escape.

He was not so lucky with the bus.

Whatever the reason—fate, or because Dunc had told him to hurry—Amos arrived at the bus stop just a half a step in front of Dunc, at the exact moment when the bus door whooshed open, and a cellular phone on the bus driver's belt rang with an incoming call.

As it turned out it was actually his wife calling to tell him to stop at the store for some cheese dip but it didn't matter.

Nothing mattered but the ring.

All the instincts kicked in and by the end of the first pulse in the first ring Amos had a foot on the bus step and was powering into the bus, left leg nailing the second step, classic form, arms pumping, hand out for the phone, a little spit flying from the side of his mouth.

Except none of this showed because he was still in deep camouflage, peering through a crack in a garbage-encrusted lampshade at the cellular phone hanging on the belt of the bus driver.

What the driver saw was terrifying. The door opened to show him a pile of banana peels and coffee grounds and bits of paper and rags and other disgusting trash suddenly come to life and come bounding up the bus steps with an appendage reaching for his belt.

He naturally slammed the bus door shut.

Or tried to. Dunc, realizing what was happening, was reaching for Amos, trying to grab him and stop him, which put his arm in the bus door as it closed. The rubber gasket kept it from cutting his arm off but did hold him firmly while inside Amos, powering into his second and important driving step, clawed for the phone on the driver's belt and missed, thrown off by running head-on into the coin and token collector.

This deflected him enough that he passed the driver completely and wound up in the front passenger seat of the bus.

The seat was not empty.

It was occupied by an older woman who had been visiting a friend on the other side of the river. The woman carried an umbrella in case it should rain. It had not rained in weeks and the umbrella had become packed and hard from not opening so that when she used it as a weapon to kill the garbage suddenly landing in her lap, she swung very hard and it was very heavy and came down with tremendous force.

Fortunately her aim wasn't that accurate so she missed Amos, except that unfortunately she aimed high and the full force of a double-gripped overhand blow brought the umbrella down on the bus driver's head, jamming his hat over his eyes.

In a reflexive action the driver jammed down on the accelerator while jerking left on the wheel. The bus took off away from the curb in a sweeping turn to the left—Dunc running alongside because his arm was caught in the door.

The sudden turn threw Amos back off the old woman toward the door. On the way he grabbed for the phone, missed again, and caught the door handle, which whooshed the door open, releasing Dunc and allowing Amos to tumble back out of the bus on top of him.

The boys rolled and stood just in time to see the bus jump the curb and come to a stop with its front window almost touching the large glass window of a Chinese restaurant.

"I think," Dunc said, "it might be time to lose our deep camouflage."

"And run," Amos added. "I just hope Melissa isn't mad because I missed her call."

Chapter · 10

"Dunc—"

"Shhh!"

It was pitch dark. Outside, the moon and stars were covered by thick clouds and the nearest surviving streetlight was four blocks away. Inside the Dumpster it was like a black hole.

"Dunc."

"You have to be quiet, Amos. We're on a mission."

"I'm hungry."

"You're what?"

"Hungry."

"We're in a Dumpster—how could you be hungry?"

"Simple. We took off this morning without eating and there wasn't much to pick up at the dump and then we did the garbage and the bus and we didn't get to eat there and when we went home and changed I fell asleep for a little bit and then you woke me up and we came down here in the dark and I was so scared I forgot about eating and now I'm hungry."

"What do you want me to do about it?"

"Nothing. I just want you to know."

"So I know. Now will you be quiet?"

"Sure."

For a moment there was silence. Then from outside the Dumpster a rasping voice hissed, "Is that you in there, garbage?"

The boys froze.

"I was worried when I gave you directions that you would leave, Mr. Garbage."

It was Charlie Rags. He had been walking since the afternoon, had spoken to several Dumpsters trying to find the talking garbage, but he hadn't had any luck except for a moment when an alley cat that looked like it had been pulled through a knothole backward snarled at him, and he thought for a second it was mad garbage.

"I need some advice, Mr. Garbage"—Charlie Rags spoke to the side of the Dumpster—"about my life."

Dunc said nothing but Amos rose to the occasion. He leaned against the inside of the Dumpster and spoke to the metal. "If I give you advice, will you go away?"

"Sure."

"What was the question?"

"Well, it's kind of complicated but now that I've stopped drinking and I'm going to straighten my life out I wondered whether I should take up the flute or be a doctor."

"Flute or doctor?"

"Yes. I was going to get on one of those television shows like Oprah and ask but I thought why should I do that when I have you? So what do you think?"

Amos thought a moment. "Do both."

"Both?"

"Yes. Be a doctor who plays a flute. Or a flute player who's a doctor."

"What a good idea. Thanks."

"Now go, and bother me no more."

Dunc had been staring at Amos in the darkness, or where Amos would be standing, and he waited until Charlie Rags's footsteps had died away. "That was great."

"What?"

"That advice. That poor old man was really worried and you helped him."

"Comes with the turf."

"What do you mean?"

"My family. My uncle Alfred is always giving advice to people who don't want it. My sister is always asking for advice and never listening to it when it comes. And—"

There was a sudden growl of an engine outside and a bump as a vehicle backed against the Dumpster.

"Quiet," Dunc whispered. He took Amos by the arm and pulled him to the opposite end of the Dumpster. "Get ready."

With a loud clang, the half-lid of the Dumpster was thrown back.

Chapter · 11

For a moment there was no sound but the running engine. Then two doors opened and slammed shut, and footsteps approached the Dumpster.

"Oh, man, one of the sacks broke, and it's all over my truck." The voice was whiny. "How come we always have to use my truck?"

"Because, pea brain, I don't *have* a truck. That's why we use your truck."

"You have a car."

"Oh, right—you want me to put bags of trash in a classic nineteen fifty-seven Chevy hardtop. Oh, really great. Perfect."

"Well—"

"That's enough whining. Now put that cigarette out before we unload this mess. Who knows what's in here?"

"It's hazardous and toxic waste—we know that. That's how come we're getting paid to dump it."

"I know that, dummy—I mean, maybe it'll catch on fire."

There was another moment of silence, after which a lit cigarette arched through the air and came spiraling into the Dumpster, where it nuzzled down into some mattress stuffing and immediately began to smolder.

"Uh-oh." Dunc whispered in Amos's ear. "This isn't so good."

"Why?" Amos spoke just above breathing.

"Nitrate—" Dunc began, then stopped as a bag of something heavy flew through the opening and burst. White powder flew in all directions, filling the Dumpster.

"No time," Dunc whispered again. "Take my hand and follow me."

"Follow you?"

"Come on." Dunc grabbed at Amos's hand and caught his wrist. *Now! It's going to blow!"*

"Blow?" Amos was still whispering. "Blow what?"

But Dunc was past talking. He slammed the length of the Dumpster dragging Amos and emerged into the open end just as another bag of white powder that had been thrown by the men hit the edge of the Dumpster and burst. Half the powder went into the Dumpster and the other half spilled back into the bed of the truck, leaving a trail of powder from the Dumpster to the truck.

Dunc pushed the torn sack off to the side and climbed up and out.

"What—" The men were standing in the back of the pickup. Around them were stacked sacks of the white powder. They were holding a sack between them, getting ready to throw it. "Who are you?" the one on the left asked.

"No time, cigarette, nitrate powder—" Dunc was gasping while he pulled at Amos to get him out of the Dumpster.

"Blow?" Amos mumbled. "What's going to blow? The garbage? How can garbage blow—"

Dunc dragged him out, across the edge of the Dumpster and onto the ground. "Now—we have to run *now!*"

63

Pulling Amos by the arm he took off at a dead run, heading across the street from the Dumpster.

The two men stood stupefied for a moment, watching the boys. Then the one who owned the truck saw smoke curling out of the Dumpster, where the cigarette was about to break into open flame.

"Fire!" he said, and jumped from the pickup bed alongside the open door of the truck. "I've got to get my truck out of here!"

He slammed the truck into gear and floored the accelerator. The truck jerked forward, throwing his partner out of the box.

It probably saved his life.

The smoldering cigarette found an edge of paper, glowed, caught, and broke into a tiny open flame. Very small, a little yellow-and-red flicker that would have died.

Except.

In an instant it found new edges of paper, caught there, grew, and was a full-blown fire just as the truck started to move.

Which was when it ignited the nitrate fertilizer.

64

Even then, for a second, it could still have been all right.

The nitrate burned but only that, just burned in a rapidly growing hot flame, feeding on itself, and growing with a great hissing. But nitrate fertilizer is just another name for explosive powder and the flames found a place where there was weight pressing down on the powder, and the pressure and flame together triggered the explosion.

Even then it might have been contained. The powder inside the Dumpster had a large opening above it, and it blew up in an enormous whooshing that lit the surrounding area like a flashbulb.

But the explosion jumped from the Dumpster to the bags stored in the back of the pickup and detonated those as well.

The effect was immediate and astonishing.

Rather than blow the pickup to pieces, the explosion was shaped toward the rear, and in a huge pulse of white-hot light, it turned the small import truck into something very close to a rocket.

A rocket aimed exactly at the front window of the Chinese restaurant.

Amos and Dunc stopped with the first explosion out of the Dumpster and turned just in time to see the pickup leave.

Or start to leave. It was much too fast to truly follow with the human eye. For one part of a second, the pickup with the polluter in the cab was sitting there, the next it was doing just under two hundred and thirty-seven miles an hour into the front window of the restaurant.

Luckily it was the middle of the night and nobody was in the restaurant except a cat named Jimmy Yee, who was just in the act of nailing a rat next to the side wall.

The pickup hit the front window exactly in the center, roared through the dining room, cored the middle of the kitchen, barreled out the back loading door, whistled through a vacant lot, caught a side street, and did not slow down for two and a half miles through the deserted streets of town, when it came to a stop in front of a police station. The man behind the wheel sat while the police came out and took him into custody. They had to carry him, still in a sitting position, into the station, where he sat in a corner and said, "I tuned

66

her up myself, but I think I got the mixture a little too rich." Then he said it again, and again, and again.

Inside the restaurant Jimmy Yee unstuck himself from the ceiling, where he'd gone as the truck came through, and dropped to the floor. The rat was gone.

"Wow." Dunc had been holding his breath. "Did you see that?"

Amos nodded. "I just hope Melissa did."

"Melissa? Why Melissa?"

"Colors," Amos said. "I never saw anything with so many colors in my life. I wonder if we can get some more of that powder."

"Amos . . ."

"Fertilizer. Is that any kind of fertilizer, or does it have to be special?" Amos started walking toward home. "I mean, you know, it's easy to get fertilizer. You can pick it up off the streets in some places. They sell it in bags in the stores. Of course, they don't call it fertilizer. Uncle Alfred calls it—"

"Amos . . ."

Be sure to join Dunc and Amos in these other Culpepper Adventures:

The Case of the Dirty Bird

When Dunc Culpepper and his best friend, Amos, first see the parrot in a pet store, they're not impressed—it's smelly, scruffy, and missing half its feathers. They're only slightly impressed when they learn that the parrot speaks four languages, has outlived ten of its owners, and is probably 150 years old. But when the bird starts mouthing off about buried treasure, Dunc and Amos get pretty excited—let the amateur sleuthing begin!

Dunc's Doll

Dunc and his accident-prone friend Amos are up to their old sleuthing habits once again. This time they're after a band of doll thieves! When a doll that once belonged to Charles Dickens's daughter is stolen from an exhibition at the local mall, the two boys put on their detective gear and do some serious snooping. Will a vicious watchdog keep them from retrieving the valuable missing doll?

Culpepper's Cannon

Dunc and Amos are researching the Civil War cannon that stands in the town square when they find a note inside telling them about a time portal. Entering it through the dressing room of La Petite, a women's clothing store, the boys find themselves in downtown Chatham on March 8, 1862—the day before the historic clash between the *Monitor* and the *Merrimac.* But the Confederate soldiers they meet mistake them for Yankee spies. Will they make it back to the future in one piece?

Dunc Gets Tweaked

Dunc and Amos meet up with a new buddy named Lash when they enter the radical world of skateboard competition. When somebody "cops"— steals—Lash's prototype skateboard, the boys are determined to get it back. After all, Lash is about to shoot for a totally rad world's record! Along the way they learn a major lesson: *Never* kiss a monkey!

Dunc's Halloween

Dunc and Amos are planning the best route to get the most candy on Halloween. But their plans change when Amos is slightly bitten by a werewolf.

Dunc Breaks the Record

Dunc and Amos have a small problem when they try hang gliding—they crash in the wilderness. Luckily, Amos has read a book about a boy who survived in the wilderness for fifty-four days. Too bad Amos doesn't have a hatchet. Things go from bad to worse when a wild man holds the boys captive. Can anything save them now?

Dunc and the Flaming Ghost

Dunc's not afraid of ghosts, although Amos is sure that the old Rambridge house is haunted by the ghost of Blackbeard the Pirate. Then the best friends meet Eddie, a meek man who claims to be impersonating Blackbeard's ghost in order to live in the house in peace. But if that's true, why are flames shooting from his mouth?

Amos Gets Famous

Deciphering a code they find in a library book, Dunc and Amos stumble onto a burglary ring. The burglars' next target is the home of Melissa, the girl of Amos's dreams (who doesn't even know that he's alive). Amos longs to be a hero to Melissa, so nothing will stop him from solving this case—not even a mind-boggling collision with a jock, a chimpanzee, and a toilet.

Dunc and Amos Hit the Big Top

In order to impress Melissa, Amos decides to perform on the trapeze at the visiting circus. Look out below! But before Dunc can talk him out of his plan, the two stumble across a mystery behind the scenes at the circus. Now Amos is in double trouble. What's really going on under the big top?